GRIMELDA
The Very Messy Witch

Peachtree

By Diana Murray

Illustrated by Heather Ross

KATHERINE TEGEN BOOKS
An Imprint of HarperCollins Publishers

Katherine Tegen Books is an imprint of HarperCollins Publishers.

Grimelda: The Very Messy Witch
Text copyright © 2016 by Diana Murray
Illustrations copyright © 2016 by Heather Ross
ISBN 978-0-06-226448-0

The artist used Photoshop to create the digital illustrations for this book.
Typography by Rachel Zegar
16 17 18 19 20   SCP   10 9 8 7 6 5 4 3 2 1
❖
First Edition

For Danny, Kate, and Jane
—D.M.

For Heidi, and her woods
—H.R.

Grimelda's house was black with grime
and stacked with jars of mold and slime,
and ogre's breath, and spotted snails,
and oozing goo in rusty pails.

Messed is best,
I always say.
That's the *proper*
witch's way.

She used her broom to fly, not sweep.
Her floors had dirt six inches deep.

But though she said she didn't mind,
sometimes things were hard to find.

"This other stuff won't do!" she said.

She tossed aside the
scream cheese spread,

the rot sauce,

and the dragon fruit.

She had to find that pickle root!

A finding spell might do the trick
if she could get her spell book quick.
But it was missing from the shelf.

I'll have to find
that root myself!

No jars of pickle root in *there*.

Not under *that*. Not *anywhere*!

Grimelda shoved her mess aside

and flung the back door open wide.

She searched the swamp out in the yard
(though all that clutter made it hard).
She found last summer's bathing suit,

but where'd I put that pickle root?

Grimelda reached inside her tree.
She found her stinkweed potpourri
and lots of other missing loot,
but *where'd* she put that pickle root?

She flew to Zelda's General Store.

She flew back home and paced the room.

She had no choice . . .

. . . She grabbed her broom.

Grimelda swept and swept some more,
as swarms of bats flew out the door.

She placed her jars in tidy rows,   then hung up all her ratty clothes.

She matched and put her socks away.
It took all night and half a day.

And while she cleaned, she found some things:

her scare spray,

witch-watch,

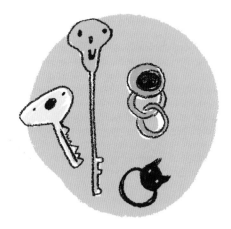

keys, and rings,

the silver buckle
from her hat,

and Wizzlewarts, her fat black cat!

She found her missing other boot
and finally . . .

And near the jar, beneath the bed,
was something else. "What's this?" she said.

She scratched her head and bent down low.

A comb? I lost this years ago!

She combed her hair.
She snagged a lump.
She pulled and pulled until—
KERFLUMP!

She shrieked, "My spell book? In my hair?
I never would have looked up there!"

Grimelda hugged the book she'd found,
then gasped and took a look around.
Her house was sparkling, neat, and clean.
The strangest sight she'd ever seen!

Grimelda knew what she must do.
She flipped to page six hundred two.

She dumped in mud
and thistle weeds,

a scoop of rotten
pumpkin seeds,

a jar of slime,

eight lumps of coal,

a pinch of toe jam
from a troll,

a puff of ogre's breath,

four fleas,

and one big slice
of moldy cheese.

She mixed and mixed the potion well,
tapped her wand, and said the spell:

Muckety-muckety, gloppety-glop,
ickety-stickety, sloppety-SLOP!

A cloud of smoke swirled up, and then . . .

. . . her house was
nice and messed again!

Grimelda breathed a happy sigh.
At last, she'd make that scrumptious pie!
She cracked the gooey egg of newt.